BY JAYNEEN SANDERS    ILLUSTRATED BY CAMILA CARROSSINE

# INCLUDED

## A BOOK FOR **ALL** CHILDREN ABOUT INCLUSION, DIVERSITY, DISABILITY, EQUALITY AND EMPATHY

BY JAYNEEN SANDERS    ILLUSTRATED BY CAMILA CARROSSINE

TO ISABELLE
THANK YOU FOR INSPIRING
THIS BOOK.

♡ J.S.

Many thanks to 'Children and Young People with Disability Australia' (CYDA)
for their invaluable advice and support. J.S.

Included
Educate2Empower Publishing an imprint of
UpLoad Publishing Pty Ltd
Victoria Australia
www.upload.com.au

First published in 2022
Text copyright © Jayneen Sanders 2022
Illustration copyright © UpLoad Publishing Pty Ltd 2022

Written by Jayneen Sanders
Illustrations by Camila Carrossine

Jayneen Sanders asserts her right to be identified as the author of this work.
Camila Carrossine asserts her right to be identified as the illustrator of this work.

Designed by Stephanie Spartels, Studio Spartels

ISBN: 9781925089752 (hbk) 9781925089790 (pbk)

A catalogue record for this
book is available from the
National Library of Australia

Disclaimer: The information in this book is advice only written by the author
based on her advocacy in this area, and her experience working with
children as a classroom teacher and mother. The information is not
meant to be a substitute for professional advice. If you are concerned
about a child's behavior seek professional help.

Everyone everywhere
wants to be included.

Everyone everywhere
wants to belong.

Our world is made up of all kinds of people.

Some people have brown hair and some people have red hair.

Some people have light skin and some people have dark skin.

Some people are shorter and some people are taller.

People's bodies look and work differently.

And people's brains work differently too.

Everyone is different. And that's okay.

What's important is that everyone feels included.

Being included makes us feel LOVED and it makes us feel SAFE.

In this book, you will learn about
six kids with disability.

You will learn a little bit about their lives.

You will also learn that these kids are
just like kids everywhere — just like you!

They love playing games, books,
making stuff and being silly.

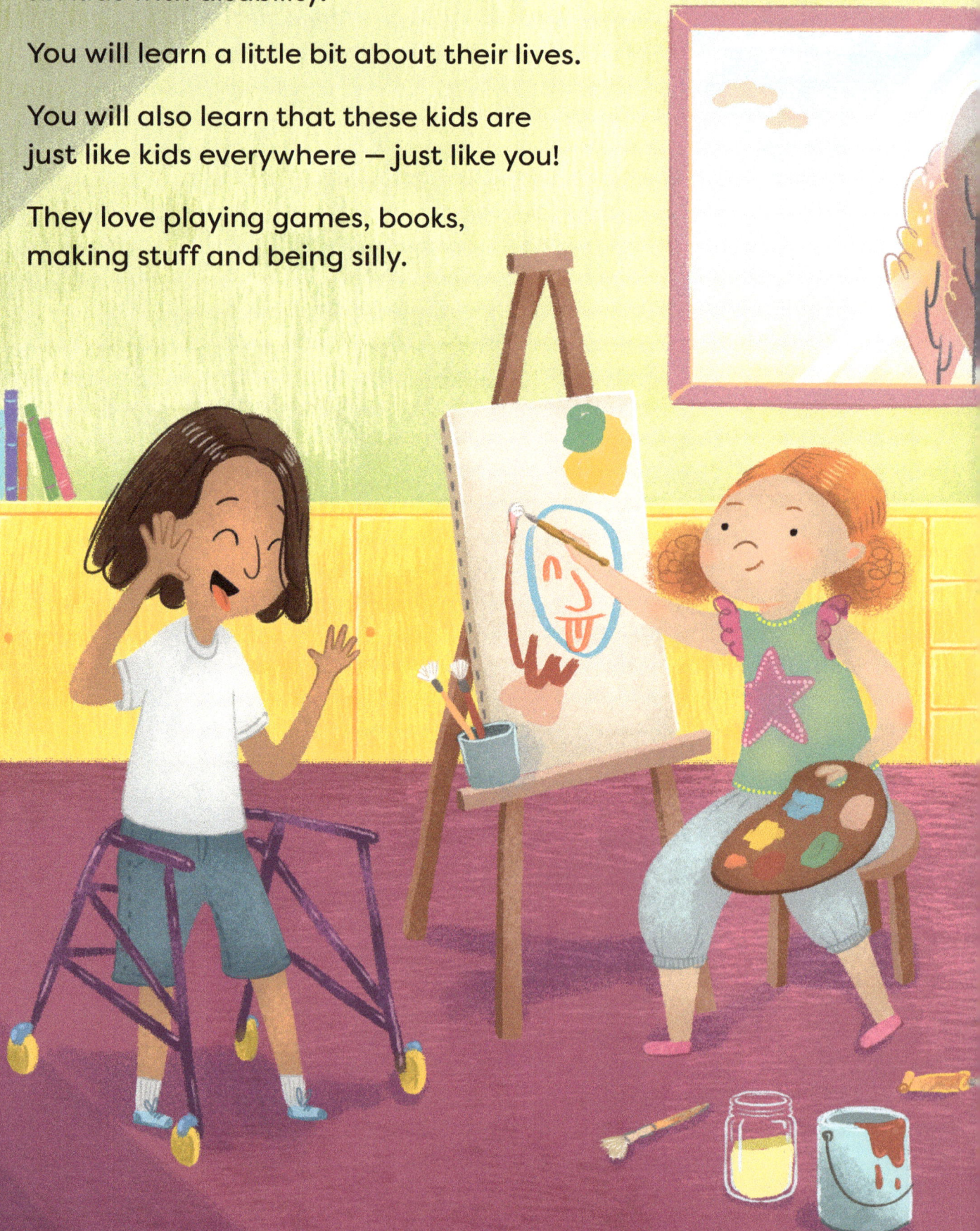

They have things they are good at, and things they are working on.

As you read this book, think about all the people you know in your community. They will have different abilities and every person will have a story.

Be curious. Ask questions and find out more. Then take your understanding and empathy out into your community, and make it a kinder and more inclusive place.

WHAT DO YOU THINK **EMPATHY** MEANS?

WHAT DO YOU THINK **INCLUSIVE** MEANS?

This is SAM.

Sam has cerebral palsy.

This means his brain developed in a different way when he was in his mother's uterus.

So, as Sam grew older, his arm and leg muscles didn't get as strong as they could have.

Sam has a community of friends and support.

He has a physiotherapist who helps his muscles to work better and get stronger.

A speech therapist to help him with his speech and his reading.

And an occupational therapist who helps him learn the skills he needs to do daily tasks — just like you have an adult who helps you learn these tasks!

WHAT DAILY TASKS DO YOU NEED TO LEARN?

Living with cerebral palsy doesn't mean Sam can't play with other kids.

Maybe the rules of a game have to change a little — but that's okay.

And maybe the other kids need to take a bit more time, so everyone knows the best way to include Sam in the game — and that's okay too!

Including Sam in any game is as simple as asking him if he'd like to play.

Sam is funny,
creative and silly.

He makes people
laugh and he makes
everyone feel included.

This is RISHI.

Rishi is autistic.

This means sometimes she sees and understands the world in a different way.

It might mean that Rishi looks away when you ask her a question. Or she might do things over and over, and over again. Sometimes a smell, a sound or food might really upset her or really interest her.

Each autistic person has their own way of seeing and understanding the world — just like you!

Rishi loves to paint. She often paints pictures of red, green and yellow.

And Rishi knows everything about dinosaurs and volcanoes.

But her favorite thing to do is to sit by the ocean and watch the waves roll in and out.

WHAT DO YOU LIKE DOING?

WHAT IS SOMETHING YOU KNOW A LOT ABOUT?

Rishi doesn't always like to be touched. And that's okay.

She can choose when she allows a person to come inside her body boundary for a hug or a handshake — just like you!

We all need to ask each other for consent before coming inside another person's body boundary.

RISHI! DO YOU WANT A HUG?

NO THANKS.

HOW ABOUT A HI-FIVE?

OKAY!

WHAT DO YOU THINK A **BODY BOUNDARY** IS?

WHAT DO YOU THINK **CONSENT** MEANS?

Sometimes Rishi loves to play with other kids. She loves to be included.

But sometimes she might choose not to join in, and that's okay. We all need to respect each other's choices.

And even though Rishi doesn't want to play, it is still important to ask her. That way she knows she can be included when she is ready.

NO, NOT TODAY.

RISHI! DO YOU WANT TO PLAY?

OKAY, NO PROBLEM.

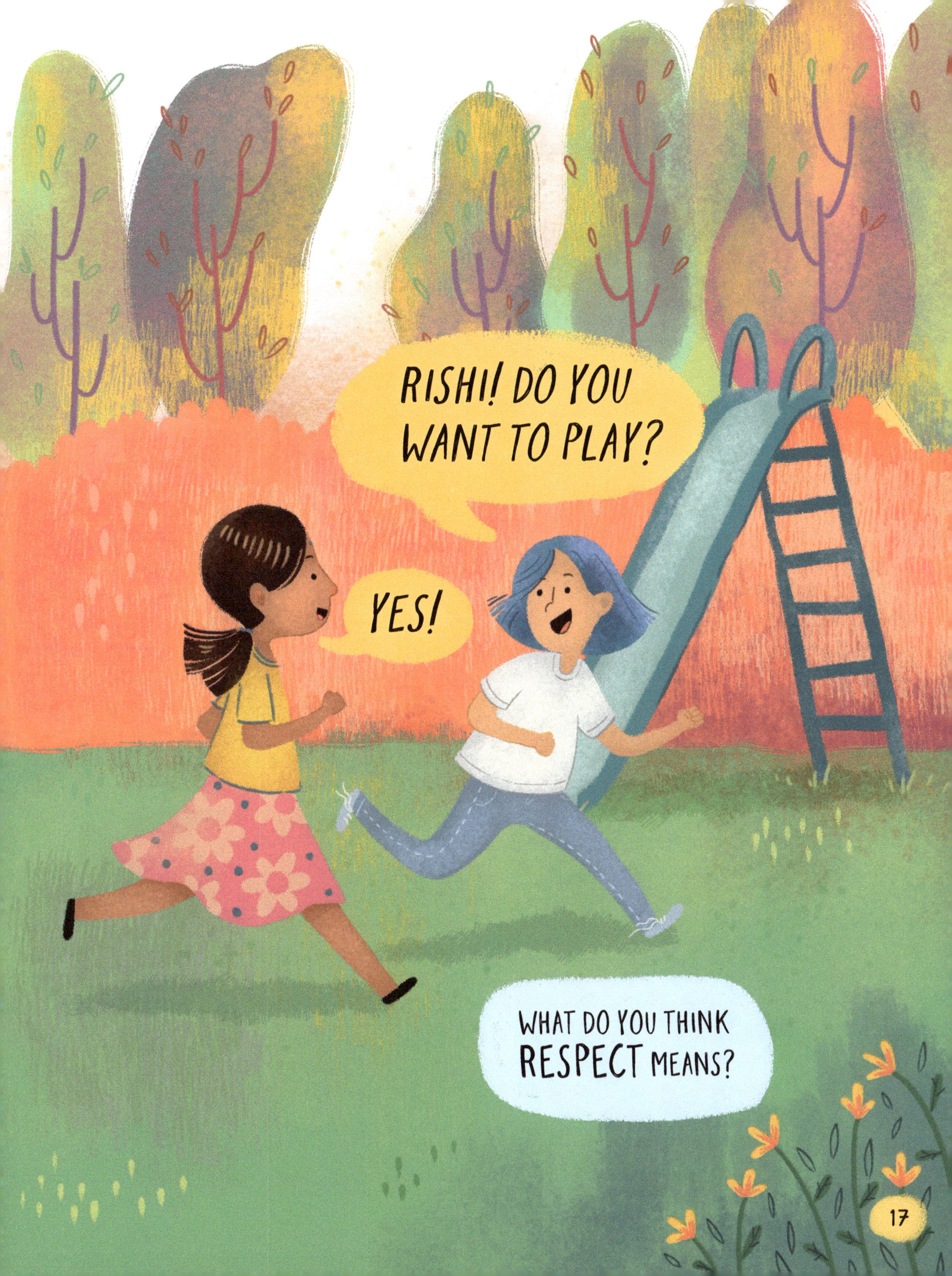

RISHI! DO YOU WANT TO PLAY?
YES!
WHAT DO YOU THINK RESPECT MEANS?

This is JAY.

Jay is deaf.

This means he can't hear the sounds around him like the TV or when his dog, Paddy, is barking.

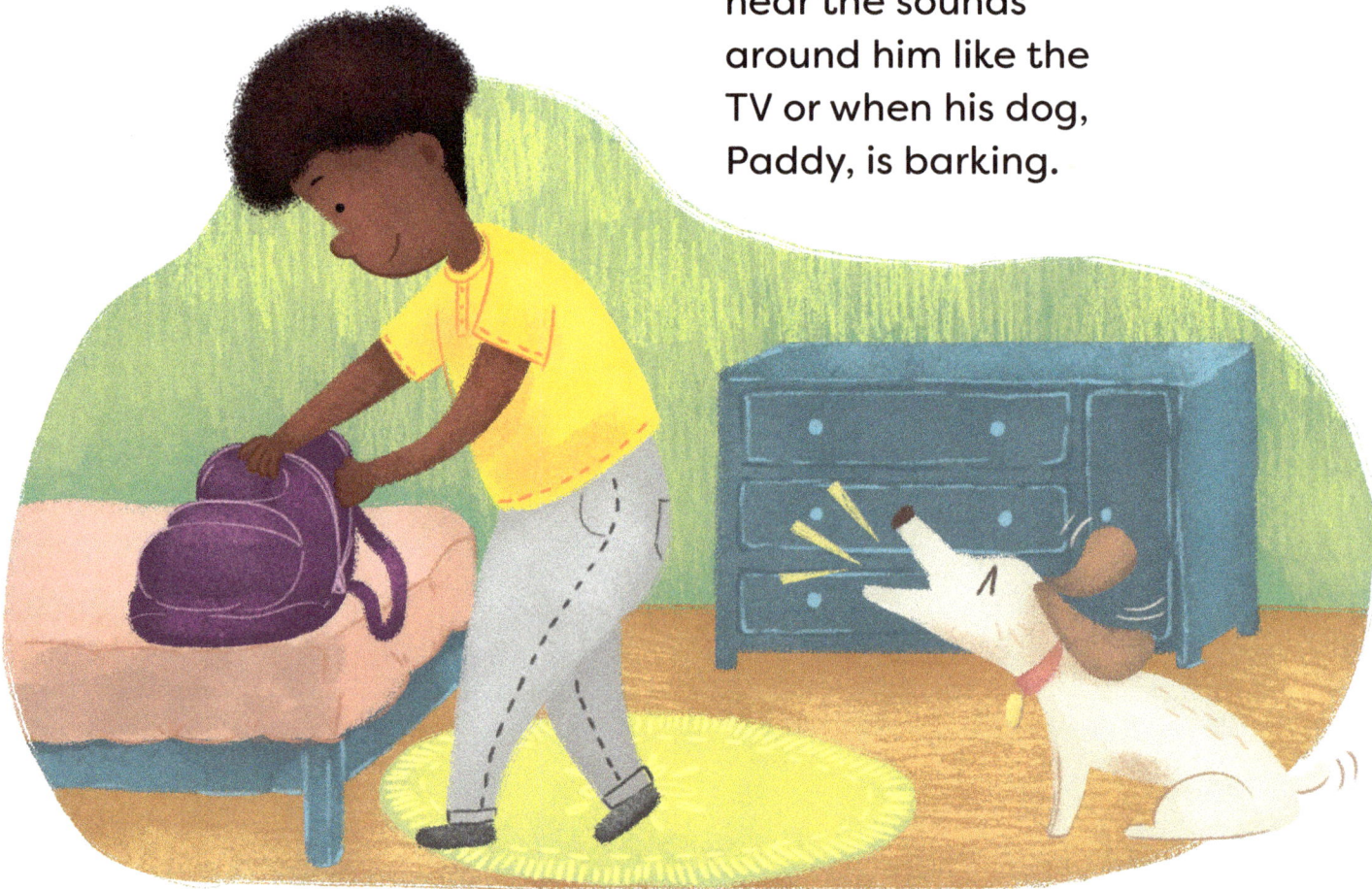

As a baby, Jay couldn't hear his parents' voices but he learned to watch their lips as they spoke to him.

Reading their lips helped him to work out what they were saying.

As Jay grew older, he learned another kind of language called sign language.

This means he 'talks' to other people through his hands and watching their faces.

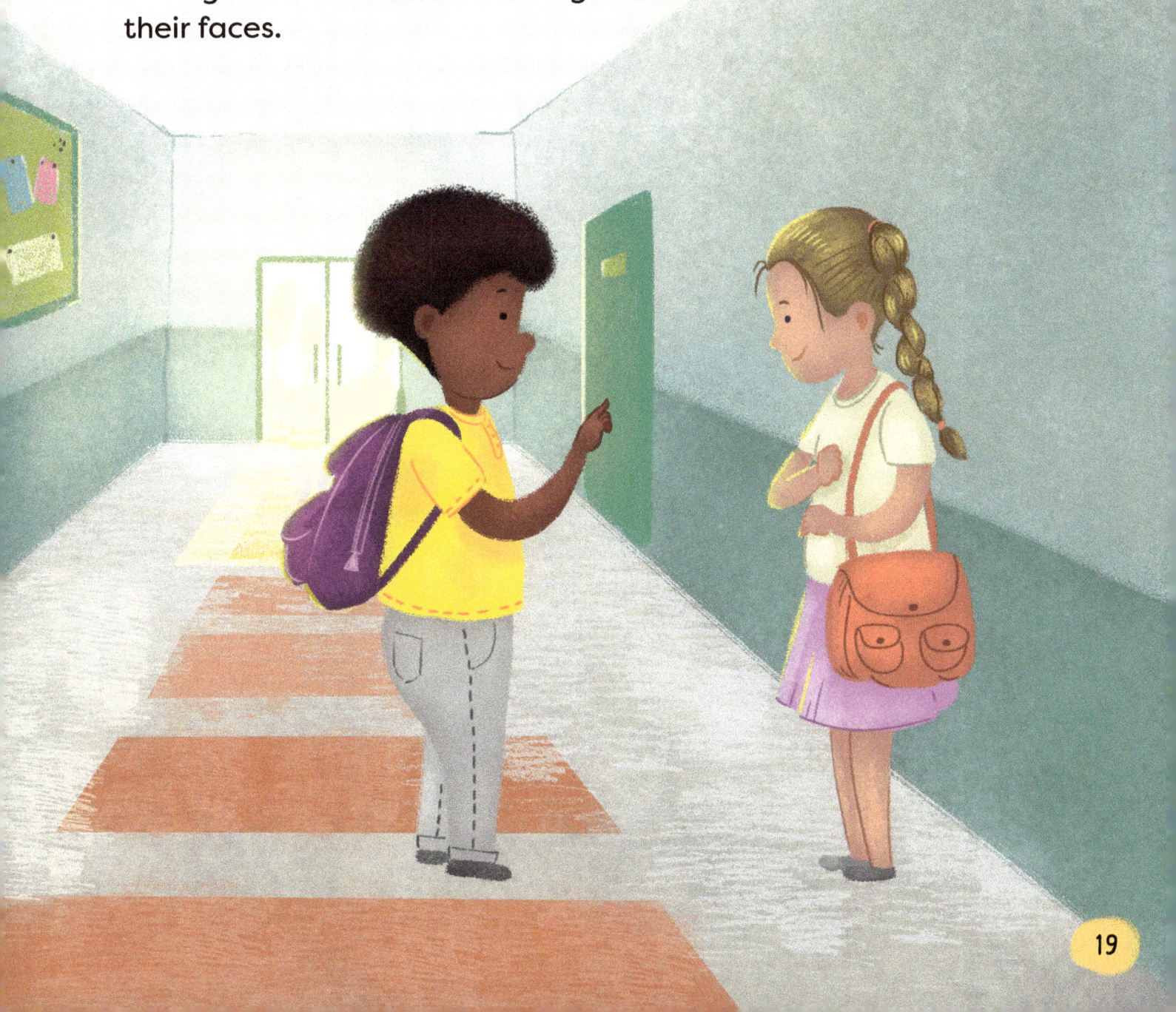

If Jay was in your class, including him in your games would be super easy.

All you would have to do is learn some sign language.

If Jay was in your class, he could teach you!

Learning sign language might be tricky to start with, but you'd soon get the hang of it! Then it would be easy for you to communicate with Jay and other people who are deaf.

Aa Bb Cc Dd

- WHAT DO YOU THINK **COMMUNICATE** MEANS?
- WHY DON'T YOU FIND OUT WHICH SIGN LANGUAGE IS USED IN YOUR COUNTRY AND LEARN SOME SIMPLE HAND SIGNALS?

This is AUDREY.

Audrey has Down Syndrome.

This means she has one more chromosome than most people.

Chromosomes are made up of genes in our body that make us who we are.

Sometimes it takes Audrey longer to learn things like counting to 100 or writing her ABCs.

And sometimes she may take longer to understand the rules of a game or how to play jump rope. But that's okay. Because Audrey's friends are always there if she needs any help.

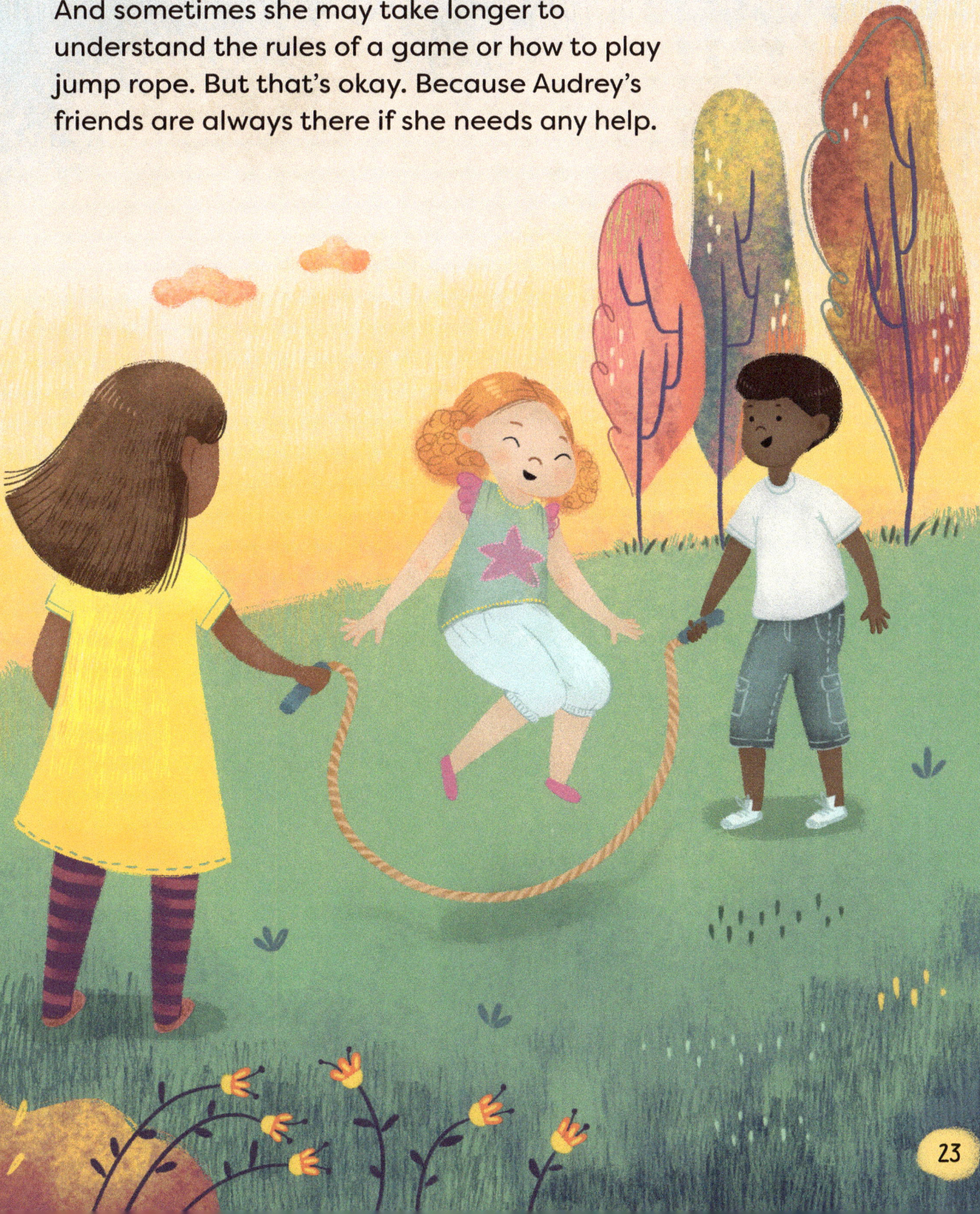

Everyone loves how happy Audrey is. Her teacher says, 'When Audrey walks into the room, the world seems brighter. She makes everyone smile.'

Audrey loves to dance. She loves to twirl and swirl, and spin around and around. Her joyful dancing encourages others to dance too.

But sometimes Audrey dances when she feels unhappy or scared. Audrey knows to tell a trusted grown-up when she feels this way.

WHO DO YOU TELL IF YOU FEEL **UNHAPPY** OR **SCARED?**

This is TY.

Ty has Attention Deficit Hyperactivity Disorder or sometimes it's called ADHD.

This means Ty has a super-duper busy brain, and a body that loves to move quickly and often.

Sometimes in the classroom, it might be hard for Ty to sit still and listen to the teacher.

Ty might need to get up and move about. They might need to play with a fidget toy or make some noise.

Ty might find it really hard to focus on a task the teacher has given to everyone.

Ty's brain and body are just very active.

The kids in Ty's class help Ty to feel included by understanding how it is for Ty.

Understanding like this is called empathy.

Sometimes Ty just needs people to show them empathy.

TY? DO YOU WANT TO READ WITH ME?

OKAY!

Mindfulness, yoga and slow breathing are some of the tools Ty can use to calm down.

These tools help all of us to slow down and quieten our minds.

Ty has learnt some important ways to calm down — so now, every day after lunch, Ty takes the class for yoga!

WHAT IS MINDFULNESS?

This is ZARA.

Zara has limb difference.

She was born without any legs below her knees.

Zara has prosthetic legs and carbon fiber blades.

Her prosthetic legs make it possible for Zara to walk and her blades make it possible for her to run.

Zara has a rainbow set of prosthetic legs for day-to-day walking and sports, and a set of blades for running.

Zara wants to go to the
Paralympics when she is older.

She wants to be part of the running team.

Zara trains very hard twice a week at
the community oval.

She is getting more confident using
her blades, and is becoming one of the
fastest runners in her age group.

At school, Zara loves basketball and football.

Everyone wants Zara on their team.

She always tries her best and is a great team player.

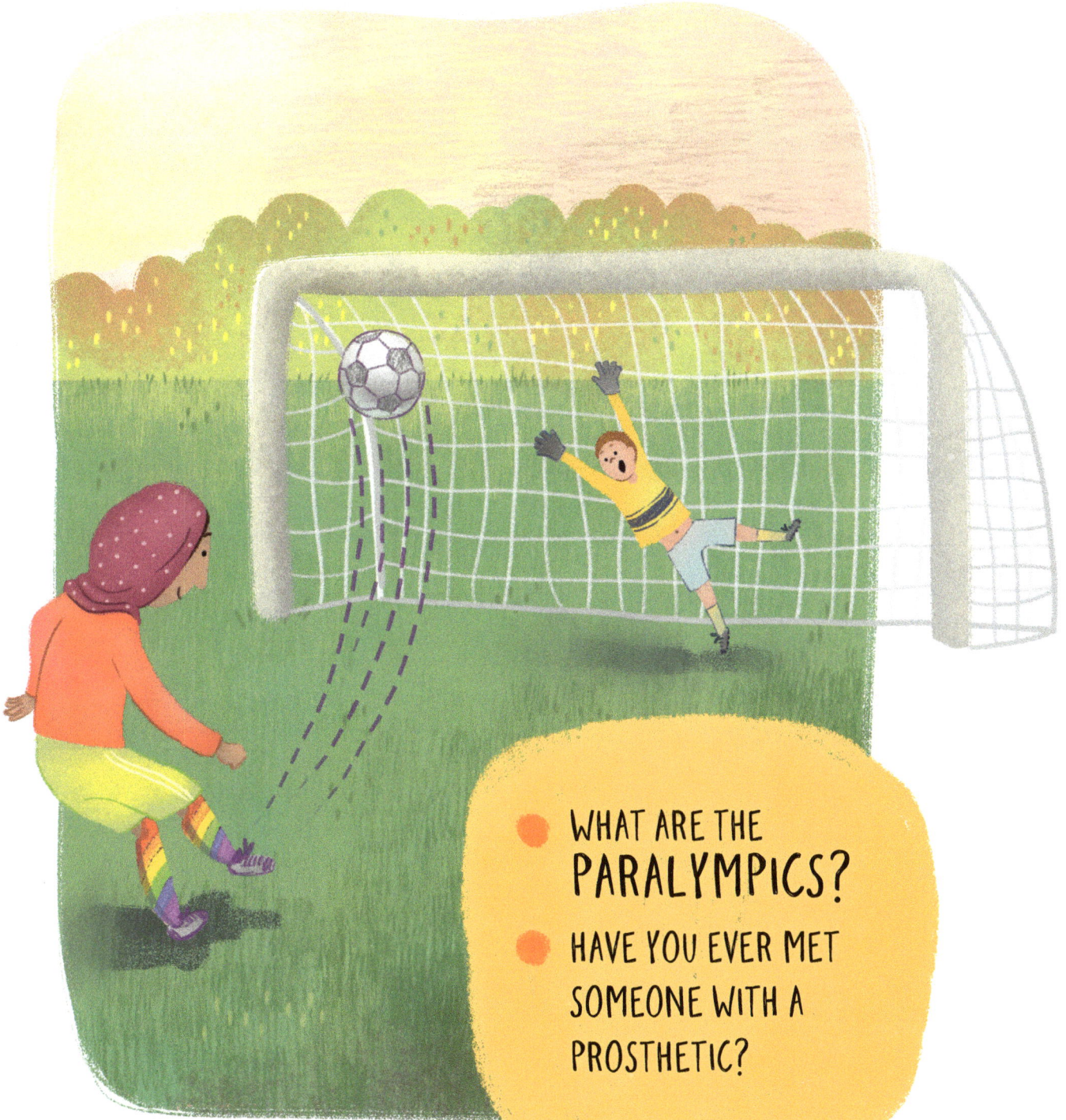

- WHAT ARE THE **PARALYMPICS?**
- HAVE YOU EVER MET SOMEONE WITH A PROSTHETIC?

Being different is okay. We are all different in our own special way.

But guess what? People are also the same.

Kids with disability are just like you.

They have things they are good at, and things they are working on.

And just like you:

- they have HOPES and DREAMS,
- they want to feel SAFE, LOVED and RESPECTED,
- and they want to feel INCLUDED.

Because everyone everywhere wants to be included.

And everyone everywhere wants to belong.

As you learn and grow you will meet all sorts of people with all sorts of abilities. Be curious!

Here are some questions to help you get a conversation going!

Remember! Good listeners listen.
They listen with curiosity and empathy.

When you ask questions, you learn more about the world and all the different kinds of people in it.

MY NAME IS _____.
WHAT'S YOUR NAME?

DO YOU WANT TO PLAY?

WOULD YOU LIKE TO JOIN IN?

WHAT IS YOUR FAVORITE:
- COLOR? WHY?
- SPORT? WHY?
- PERSON? WHY?
- PET? WHY?
- ANIMAL? WHY?
- THING TO DO? WHY?
- THING TO DO AT SCHOOL? WHY?

# DISCUSSION QUESTIONS
## FOR PARENTS, CAREGIVERS AND EDUCATORS

The following questions are a guide only. They can be used at the time of the first reading, or at a later reading where you and your child take time to discuss the illustrations and text in more detail. **Note:** this book can be read over a number of sessions. The questions below will help you to unpack some of the ideas around inclusion and disability with your child. The aim of this book is to encourage a generation of children to be 'upstanders' and 'includers' both now and into their futures, so our world becomes a more inclusive and kinder place.

**Pages 4–5**
**Note:** take time to discuss each concept on these pages, e.g. Ask, 'Who has brown hair in our family? How is my body different to yours?' Ask, 'How are you different to me/xxxx? (Add anyone's name here.) How are we the same? How are you the same as xxxx? Do you always feel included at school/dance/swimming, etc? Why do you say that? How does feeling "included" make you feel? How might it feel to not be included in a game or activity?'

**Pages 6–7**
Ask, 'What do you think the word "disability" means?' **Note:** gain your child's general understanding of the term at this point. Ask, 'What do you like doing? What things are you good at? What things are you working on? Who do you know in your community? Do you know anyone with disability? Why don't we ask them about their life and their story?' **Note:** only if the person suggested has been asked if they are comfortable sharing their life story. Ask, 'How might you and I make the world a kinder place?'

**Pages 8–9**
Ask, 'Do all the kids look like they are having fun? Why do you say that? What do you think a physiotherapist/speech therapist/ occupational therapist does?' **Note:** you could stop your reading at this point and explain, in general terms, what these

therapists do. Ask, 'What are some daily tasks you had to learn as you grew older? Who helped you to learn these tasks?'

**Pages 10–11**
Ask, 'Would you like to play with Sam? If you saw Sam in the playground what might you do?' Say, 'That's right. You could include him in your game or he might include you in his game. You could learn things about each other by asking each other questions.' Ask, 'What do you think "creative" means?'

**Pages 12–13**
Ask, 'What is your favorite thing to do? Is there anything you know a lot about? Why don't you show or tell me all about it? Do you have any friends who are autistic? What games do you play together?'

**Pages 14–15**
Ask, 'How do you like to greet people? Do you change your mind in how you greet people sometimes? What is a body boundary?' Say, 'That's right! It is the invisible space around your body; and just because it's invisible that doesn't mean it isn't there.' Ask, 'What do you think "consent" means? Who needs to ask for your consent before coming inside your body boundary? Do medical people also need to ask for your consent before coming inside your body boundary or touching your body?' Say, 'Yes, that's right. They absolutely do!'

**Pages 16–17**
Ask, 'What do you think "respect" means?'
Say, 'That's right. It means listening to
other's wishes and points of view with
understanding.' Ask, 'Do you always have
to play with someone if they ask you?' Say,
'That's right. You can say "No" but try to say
it kindly and thank them for asking.' Ask,
'What are some of the choices you make?'

**Pages 18–19**
Ask, 'Have you ever been taught sign
language? What did you learn?'

**Pages 20–21**
Ask, 'What do you think "communicate"
means?' Say, 'Different countries use
different sign language. Maybe you could
find out which sign language is used in your
country. You could learn some words and
letters, and share what you know with your
family and/or class.'

**Pages 22–23**
Say, 'Genes and the chromosomes in
our body make us who we are.' Ask,
'Would you like to find out more about
genes and chromosomes?' **Note:** if your
child is interested in the topic, encourage
or help them to do some research.
Ask, 'How do your friends help you?
How do you help your friends?'

**Pages 24–25**
Ask, 'What do you do if you feel unhappy or
scared?' **Note:** explain a 'trusted grown-up'
as an adult that makes them feel safe and
believes them when they express concerns.
Ask, 'Do you like to dance? How does it
make you feel? Sometimes people worry
that others will laugh at them when they
dance; should we worry about something
like that?' Say, 'That's right! We should just
be ourselves and if we love to dance or sing,
we should do it. Just like Audrey!'

**Pages 26–27**
Ask, 'Do you ever find it hard to focus?
What do you do if this happens?' **Note:**
'they' and 'them' are used as Ty's gender-
neutral pronouns.

**Pages 28–29**
Ask, 'What do you think "empathy" means?
How is the girl helping Ty? Have you ever
done yoga? Did you enjoy it? Can you show
me any yoga poses you know? What is
mindfulness?' Say, 'That's right. Mindfulness
means to spend time quietly noticing all
the things around you in that moment and
feeling calm.' Ask, 'Is there a place that
makes you feel really calm? Where is it?
What could you do if you were feeling like Ty
and your busy brain just won't slow down?'

**Pages 30–31**
Ask, 'What do you think "limb difference"
means?' Say, 'That's right. A person is
missing a limb or a number of limbs, and
may use prosthetics, or they were born with
a limb that is a different shape or size.'
**Note:** you may need to explain a prosthetic
as a replacement body part constructed
from human-made materials.

**Pages 32–33**
Ask, 'What are the Paralympics? Have you
ever watched or been to the Paralympics?'
Say, 'Let's find out more about the sports
the Paralympians participate in?' Ask, 'What
do you think "confident" means? What can
you do with confidence? What qualities
might a "great team player" have?'

**Pages 34–35**
Say, 'Let's write down all the things that
are the same and all the things that are
different about you and me.' Ask, 'What are
you good at? What things are you working
on? What are your hopes and dreams?
Do you feel safe/loved/respected/included?
Why do you say that?'

**Pages 36–37**
**Note:** encourage your child to be curious
and to be an 'inclusive' person where they
go out of their way to include all children
in their games, conversations and life in
general! Promote being an 'upstander'
not a 'bystander' and being an 'includer'
not an 'excluder'.

# BOOKS BY THE SAME AUTHOR

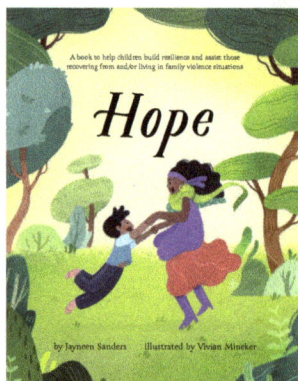

## HOPE

This beautifully illustrated book will provide children in family violence homes with a sense of hope and to lessen the traumatic effects of their living situations. Discussion Questions included. Ages 6 to 12 years.

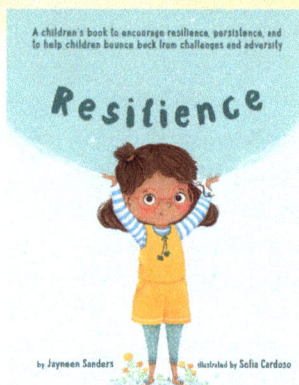

## RESILIENCE

This charming story about a little girl called Emmi uses verse and familiar childhood scenarios to encourage children to be resilient, persistent, and to help them bounce back from challenges and adversity. Discussion Questions included. Ages 4 to 9 years.

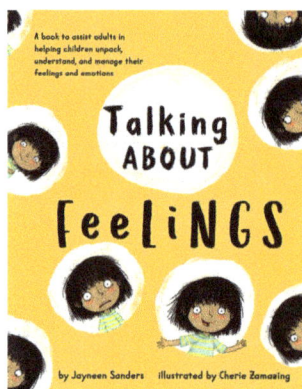

## TALKING ABOUT FEELINGS

A book to assist adults in helping children to unpack, understand, and manage their feelings and emotions in an engaging and interactive way. Discussion Questions included. Ages 4 to 10 years.

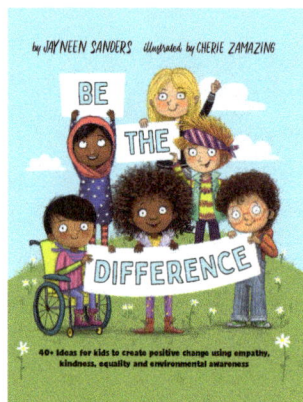

## BE THE DIFFERENCE

This engaging book provides over 40 powerful ideas on how kids can make a difference. It focuses on three key areas: empathy and kindness, racial and gender equality, and the environment. Discussion Questions included. Ages 5 to 12 years.

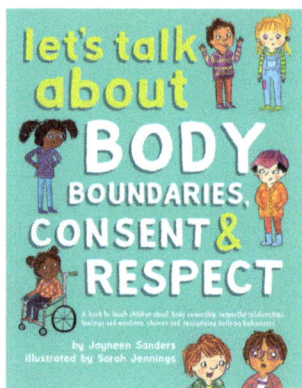

## LET'S TALK ABOUT BODY BOUNDARIES, CONSENT AND RESPECT

Through familiar scenarios, this book opens up crucial conversations with children around consent and respect. Discussion Questions included. Ages 4 to 10 years.

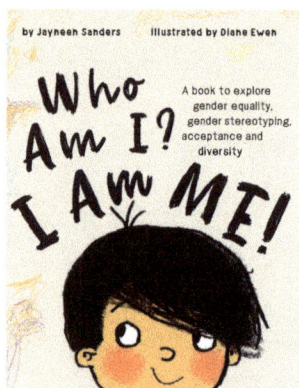

## WHO AM I? I AM ME!

This story explores gender equality and gender stereotyping through an engaging character called Frankie. Frankie illustrates that it doesn't matter if you identify as a girl or a boy; we should be free to be ourselves. Discussion Questions and tips for gender-neutral parenting and teaching included. Ages 3 to 8 years.

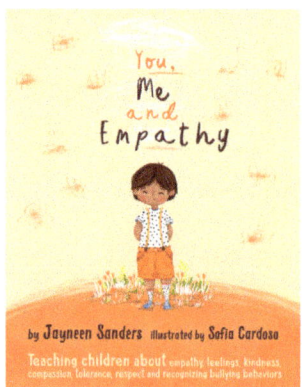

## YOU, ME AND EMPATHY

This charming story uses verse, beautiful illustrations and a little person called Quinn to model the meaning of empathy, kindness and compassion. Discussion Questions and activities to promote empathy and kindness included. Ages 3 to 9 years.

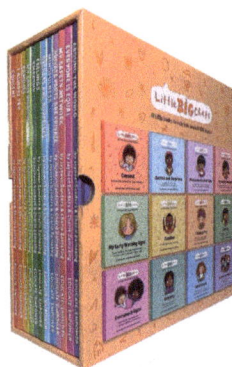

## LITTLE BIG CHATS SERIES

This series has been written to help parents, carers and teachers initiate age-appropriate conversations with early learners around crucial, and yet at times, 'tough' topics such as body safety, gender equality and diversity. Discussion Questions included. Ages 2 to 6 years.

FOR MORE INFORMATION GO TO: WWW.E2EPUBLISHING.INFO